This book is dedicated to Cooper, Amaia and
Éabha, and all children around the world helping
to keep Colin safely away from animals and the
wild places where he doesn't belong.

Published in the UK by Scholastic, 2022
Euston House, 24 Eversholt Street, London, NW1 1DB
Scholastic Ireland, 89E Lagan Road, Dublin Industrial Estate, Glasnevin, Dublin, D11 HP5F

SCHOLASTIC and associated logos are trademarks and/or
registered trademarks of Scholastic Inc.

Text © Sarah Roberts, 2022
Illustrations © Hannah Jayne Lewin, 2022

ISBN 978 0702 30832 1

A CIP catalogue record for this book is available from the British Library.

Printed in Italy by L.E.G.O. S.p.A.
This book by Scholastic is made of material from well-managed,
FSC®-certified forests and other controlled sources.

1 3 5 7 9 10 8 6 4 2

www.scholastic.co.uk

SOMEBODY CRUNCHED COLIN

SARAH ROBERTS

Illustrated by

HANNAH JAYNE LEWIN

SCHOLASTIC

Down in the leafy green garden,
Colin lay scrunched on the ground.
He longed to be like the sweet flowers,
to catch someone's eye and be found.

Animals hovered around him
as his scent drifted on the fresh air.
Colin smelt very alluring,
but no one knew why he was there.

You see, Colin didn't belong on the floor.

Out of nowhere a **bandit** came creeping,
in a sneaky black mask with striped tail.
Quietly she crawled down the tree trunk,
and followed the smell of the trail.

She ducked in and out of the shadows,
her little legs running so fast,

with her nose in the air as she travelled,
until she found Colin at last.

The **raccoon** ran away clutching Colin,
she wanted to try a small taste.

When suddenly Colin went **CRACKLE!**
And the masked bandit dropped him with haste.

Colin sat wrinkled and crinkled
in a jumble of crispy brown leaves.
Inquisitive **butterflies** hovered
as his tasty scent sailed on the breeze.

But Colin didn't belong in the leaves.

Before long, **a big grizzly stranger**,
was searching for something to eat.

His nose sniffed and snuffled round Colin
as he smelt a most flavoursome treat!

The **bear** pawed at Colin and grunted,
his shiny snack seemed very odd.

He **scrunched** him and **crunched** him and
and struggled to **munch** him,
then gave up ... and off the bear trod.

Colin felt more lost than ever,
as the wind made him shudder and shiver.
A sudden great gust blew and grabbed him,
and pushed him - **SPLASH!** - into the river.

But Colin didn't belong in the water.

He WHIRLED and he SWIRLED with the current, twisting and turning so fast!

Then Colin got into a tangle when a SLIPPERY SWIMMER sped past.

The **otter** was struggling to swim –
she couldn't release her trapped paw!

Then a **WAVE** suddenly caught hold of Colin,
and he **CRASHED!** in a spray on the shore.

Though he was soggy and crumpled,
Colin still sparkled and shone.
And just like the **flowers** he admired so,
the allure of his smell carried on.

But Colin didn't belong on the shore.

Colin glinted and caught more attention
as a **Sharp-eyed COLLECTOR** flew by.

Swiftly she swooped down to grab him
and lifted him up to the sky.

The **bird** flew away in an instant
with Colin gripped in her small beak.

As an **eagle** launched down without warning, the **small bird** let out a great **SHRIEK!**

Colin now **FLICKERED** and **FLUTTERED**
as he drifted back down to the ground,
where a furry friend bounded straight
over and barked at what he had found.

Wagging his tail excitedly,
he slobbered and sniffed with delight.

The **dog** leant in to lick Colin,
and his shiny, wet nose got **stuck tight**.

His shaggy fur shook as he panicked,
the **frightened dog** let out a whine.

Unable to breathe, he didn't feel good,
but a kind hand reached down just in time.

Looking at Colin, a **friendly voice** said,

"You don't belong here on the floor!
There's a **Special bin** here where I'll place you,
so you can be useful once more."

Back in the **leafy green garden**,
with the song of the birds and the bees,

the child picked up Colin ... the **watering can!** ...
and they watered the flowers and trees.